I Go Ape!

by

BRIAN MOSES

First published in Great Britain in 2014
by Caboodle Books Ltd
Copyright © Brian Moses

A Catalogue record for this book is available
from the British Library.

ISBN 978 095694829 8

Cover Illustration by Chris White
Page Layout by Highlight Type Bureau Ltd
Printed by CPI Group (UK) Ltd, Croydon, CR0 4YY

The paper and board used in the paperback by
Caboodle Books Ltd are natural recyclable products
made from wood grown in sustainable forests.
The manufacturing processes conform to the environmental
regulations of the country of origin.

Caboodle Books Ltd
Riversdale, 8 Rivock Avenue, Steeton, BD20 6SA
www.authorsabroad.com

Dedication:

For the staff and pupils at
Heathlands Primary School, Bournemouth
where I am currently their Patron of Reading.

Contents

I Go Ape

When I hang upside down, I'm orang-utang,
when I climb a tree, I'm chimpanzee,
when I'm tough as Attila, you can call me gorilla,
but to keep in shape, I go ape.

I go, I go, I go ape,
I go, I go, I go ape.

oo oo oo oo oo oo oo oo!

I'm with people of every size and shape
looking for adventure and going ape,
leaving the streets and leaving the town
for the joys of hanging upside down.

I wanna let all my energy escape,
like a marathon runner reaching the tape,
show everybody how fit I can be,
I wanna release the hidden monkey in me
and go ape.

I go, I go, I go ape,
I go, I go, I go ape.

oo oo oo oo oo oo oo oo!

If there's no pain, there can be no gain,
maybe I could be Tarzan, you could be Jane,
swinging so high we could hang from the stars,
slide Saturn's rings and cartwheel on Mars.

When I hang upside down, I'm orang-utang,
when I climb a tree, I'm chimpanzee,
when I'm tough as Attila, you can call me gorilla,
but to keep in shape, I go ape.

I go, I go, I go ape,
I go, I go, I go ape.

oo oo oo oo oo oo oo oo!

Nobody Loves a Maggot

Nobody wants to tickle
a maggot under it's chin.
Nobody yells, 'Hooray,'
I've got maggots in my bin.

Nobody whispers secrets
into a maggot's ear.
Nobody says, 'Get the party started
now that the maggot's here'.

A maggot is not an honoured guest,
someone to welcome in.
A maggot's place can only be
inside a smelly bin.

Maggots are shunned, unspoken of
and generally ignored.
Nothing much for maggots to do
so they probably get bored.

They don't feature on television,
they're never heroes in a book.
A maggot's public appearance
is pinned to a fishing hook.

Like nature's other irritants,
wasps and slugs and fleas,
nobody loves a maggot
or wants to give one a squeeze.

So should we declare a day
when maggots are really cool.
A 'National Maggot Day'
with slogans like 'Maggots Rule.'

Or should we just pretend
that maggots don't exist.
If maggots disappeared
then surely they wouldn't be missed?

The Rat is Back

The rat is back,
gnawing away at our fragile defences
with the kind of midnight noise
that's amplified in the darkness,
leading us to believe
that we might be under attack
from an army of rats.
No one feels safe in the garden now,
the children stay indoors,
watch from the window
for rat to appear.
Vague memories return
of history lessons -
how the plague spread -
we want the rat dead.
It won't take a hint,
it won't go away.
I come home each day -
how are you all, how's the rat?
This creature of midnight,
now brazen in daylight -
makes no attempt to hide.
It grows bigger on
stolen rabbit food,
and if I set a trap,
it ignores it.
I fear that we'll see it soon,
swollen to enormous size,
and hear it chitchat-chattering
as it batters down our door.

Let's Hear it for
the Dung Beetle

For far too long, the dung beetle
has been an unsung hero.
Nobody writes songs about dung beetles,
nobody says how great they are
or wants to be bezzie mates with one.
Dung beetles are not considered cool,
nobody scrawls, 'Dung Beetles Rule'
on walls around our towns and cities.
Dung beetles are simply shunned,
they merely do their thing with dung,
day in, day out, roll it about.
But what puzzles me is don't they ever
want to try out something new.
Ice cream maybe, or a vindaloo,
chocolate, chips or pizza slices.
Surely anything's got to be better
than a constant diet of POO!

Squirrel

A clatter of claws
signals her arrival,
the line of our fence
her expressway -
a route along which to scoot,
to shoot, to chase, to race
with the male on her tail.
And then later she's back,
squirreling her stuff away,
forgetting where she buries it,
the maps in her head all wrong.

But I wish I could be like her,
a tightrope walker on the telephone wire.
I could leave my home and aerial walk
to the house across the street.
That would be neat.....

The Cows

They came with the swallows, when frost
still patterned the ground & the first
visitors aired their caravans.
They were nervous, then curious,
then playful.

All summer they hoovered the grass
or trailed my wife as she crossed the field,
like a line of hired detectives
hard on her heels.

Each evening their rough flanks jostled
for space, like rugby forwards at a huge
scrum down, broad backs packing
a patch by the road.

But today I noticed the cows were missing.
Something must have spirited them away
through the gate on the far side.

I felt bad about seeing them leave,
had, over the past months, struck up
an easy relationship with them.

We passed the time of day,
me trying to engage them in conversation:
The weather, flies, the nutrient value of hay,

as they looked at me with doleful eyes,
giving me their attention for at least
ten seconds till more pressing thoughts
turned them back to grass.

The cows and I got along OK
and now I don't like to think
where it is that they've gone.

Freddie Cannon

Freddie Cannon
always goes off with a BANG!
He's the sort of boy who always fails
to get the hang of things,
even simple things like
putting one foot in front of the other.
But Freddie's a blast to be with,
to rock along the road together,
watching him, hopping, ducking and diving,
desperately trying to avoid
the inevitable collisions
with passers by.

He's great Freddie, he's a mate,
but I hate it when he says
the wrong thing. In class,
in the lunch queue, or when any sort of
interruption is clearly the last thing
that's needed, Freddie jumps in.
Like the ack ack of an angry gun,
his opinions spat out like shrapnel.
Devastating dramas talked about
for months, with Freddie banned
from breaktime, and all his favourite
activities.

Maybe he'll learn in time or
maybe he's on a collision course
with life as he knows it.

And me? I'm on the outside
looking in, too timid to copy
Freddie's example, destined to fly
in his slipstream, rocked by his world
but safe in his shadow.
Glad it's not me who's
Freddie Cannon,
but glad that Freddie's
my friend.

Who Did It?

"Who drew tattoos on the cavemen,
just who has been misbehaving?
And who stuck plasters on Guy Fawkes
so he looks like he's cut himself shaving?

And who on earth added nose rings
to Henry VIII and his wives,
who's being so disrespectful
to all these historical lives?

And who tucked a mobile phone
under Florence Nightingale's chin?
Who dared to be so impolite
to our national heroine?

Who added rocket boosters
to a Roman chariot race?
And who pencilled in a moustache
on Queen Victoria's face?

Somebody better own up,
we'll be staying here till they do."
Then our teacher looked
straight at me,
"I bet I'm right - it was **YOU!**"

Miss Maybury

Our teacher said, Miss Maybury
would surely blow her top.
"You really have annoyed her,
you should have known when to stop."

Miss Maybury may be colour blind
but one colour she sees is red.
'You'll wish you never came to school,"
is what our teacher said.

If someone tried to measure
the scale of Miss Maybury's rage
it would feature on a chart
that disappeared off the page.

We've heard her yell and scream
like a fearsome fiend from hell.
She's practised an awful lot
and she does it very well.

Steam streams from her ears,
her reputation's volcanic.
Her outbursts are legendary
her stamina titanic.

There's nothing now to do
but tremble and quiver with fear,
wishing that we were anywhere,
anywhere but here.....

A Time Eraser

Wouldn't it be great
to be able to roll back time
and re-visit what we were,
to make amends for what we did wrong,
to refashion what we've become,
get rid of those cringe-making moments
with one stroke of an eraser?

Wouldn't it be great if life was just a first draft?
Like a piece of writing that you could go back
and tidy up before you presented it.
Hurtful words could be removed,
more sensitive sentences inserted.

I'd love to be able to cut and paste my life,
to lose the daft bits, the sad bits,
the excruciatingly awful bits.
That girl I asked for a date and she said no.
In the revised life that I devised
she'd immediately agree.
And that ball I kicked through the window
could be booted back, with the window unbroken,
not even a crack.

That easy question I fluffed in the maths lesson,
letting the teacher know that I knew absolutely
nothing at all. No worries now,
a quick flick will rub it out and get rid
of my red face.

Wouldn't it be great to do all that,
to just wind back and change the days,
to give myself a good-as-new life,
one that wouldn't embarrass me.

(Anyone lend me that sort of eraser,
I'd really be very grateful?)

I'd Rather be Doing Anything today than.......

I'd rather be doing anything today
than going to school.

I'd rather tightrope walk across Grand Canyon.
or tumble over Niagara Falls in a barrel.

I'd rather have my feet nibbled by piranhas.
or try to tiptoe past a sleepy lion.

I'd rather eat brussel sprouts for my birthday tea.
or bungee jump from the Empire State Building.

I'd rather wander through the town in my underwear.
or practise juggling with dynamite.

I'd rather kiss a pot bellied pig.
or sleep in a nest of vipers.

I'd rather walk through a haunted forest at night.
or be invited to tea at Dracula's Castle.

I'd rather have a spitting contest with a camel
or be forced to eat sardine sandwiches.

Yes, I'd rather be doing anything today
than going to school...

Because school's just not cool enough
for me.

(I'm sure you can add other ideas to this yourself......)

A Sick Room

(For everyone in the junior school at Sutton High.)

I found a sick room
in a school that I visited
and wondered how long
the room had been unwell.

It must be a very sick room
because Anna said the room had been ill
from the day she first started school.

I hope it was being looked after.
Perhaps everyone passes by quietly,
keeping the noise down
so not to wake the room from its sleep.

Maybe the room has visiting hours
where children can call and offer
grapes and good wishes.

Maybe there's a daily bulletin
as to how the room is feeling.
Perhaps cards are sent, 'Hey room,
hope you're better soon.'

Or is the door locked
so no one can go inside.
Maybe the room's contagious,
the walls broken out in spots,
the ceiling sneezing.

All the other rooms looked healthy enough,
bright and cheerful.

Maybe next time I visit
this very sick room will have made
a complete recovery.

Paradise Street

Paradise Street in our town
was a street you didn't go down.

All the boys I was warned not to play with
lived on Paradise Street.

All the boys who swore,
who wore scars like fashion accessories,
who didn't need a reason to beat you up
or knock you down,
they all lived on Paradise Street.

Each season, a different torture.
In winter it was snowballs with sharp icy hearts,
In spring, they'd fling frogspawn.
Summer they dropped water bombs,
Autumn they were deadly with conkers.

Bogeymen. werewolves, vampires, the undead,
all the nightmares I dreaded
all started on Paradise Street.

Paradise Street was a short cut
that nobody took,
where nobody went at night.

The lights were all smashed
on Paradise Street,
it was doubly dangerous in the dark.

And when I think back
to Paradise Street,
I wonder who it was who gave it
such a crazy name.

Paradise Street
wasn't paradise
for anyone I knew.

Pleasant Street

(For everyone at VCP, the school on Pleasant Street in Jersey)

How pleasant to live on Pleasant Street
where nobody gets annoyed,
where news is always good
and the residents overjoyed
to live in such a street
where raised voices are seldom heard,
where arguments never happen
and no one speaks a cross word.

There are no takers in Pleasant Street
for everyone learns how to give.
No one ever moves from Pleasant Street
for where else could they live?
Once you've seen the warmth of its welcome,
once you've felt the sun on your shoulder,
once you've found out how young you stay
and how nobody grows any older.

I'd love to live on Pleasant Street
where no one complains about money,
where happiness spreads like sunshine
and gleams like golden honey.
For everyone here knows that laughter
is really good for your health.
To offer the gift of laughter shows
a special kind of wealth.

How pleasant to see smiles everywhere
and nobody wearing a frown.
I'd love to discover Pleasant Street
in every city and town.

(Is There Anything to do in) Wickhambreaux?

Is it scary
in Wickhambreaux?
What do you do
when you want excitement
in Wickhambreaux?
Do you abseil
down the church tower
or scuba dive
in the village pond?
Do you roll down
the roofs of thatched cottages,
first making sure
there's something soft to catch you
when you land?
Do you pole vault the power lines
between pylons
or play football in a field
where there's a bull?
Well, what do you do
in Wickhambreaux
and where on earth
do you do it?
Beats me!

(Wickhambreaux, pronounced *Wickham-brew*,
is a small village in Kent.)

Piecing Together the Perfect Christmas

To begin with
you come across the pieces by chance -
a twinkle of tinsel in a shop window,
a Christmas song on the radio.
Soon afterwards you realise
that there's some connection
with the string of lights that flash
from your neighbour's garage
and the tops of pine trees
that loll around outside greengrocers.
Then the pieces are quick to reveal themselves.
One Santa's grotto slides into
holly wreaths and a Salvation Army band
playing carols on a Saturday.
The picture grows clearer
as parcels, decorations, cards all interlink
although some pieces are harder to find,
like the presents you tuck away
out of sight from prying eyes.
Then it's Christmas Eve and the picture
is shaping up; only a few more pieces to discover.
And you search and search but they can't be found.
And you know that they must be out there somewhere,
in the night sky, in the holy lands,
out there with the angels
amid the architecture of stars.
And if you knew what they were
you could put them in place,
until the picture became perfect.

So each Christmas you search,
each Christmas you hope
that you're piecing together
the perfect Christmas,
that this year will be
the one.

That Magic of Christmas Day

If only we could have trapped it,
that magic of Christmas Day,
or stretched it like elastic
for a few more hours
into Boxing Day.
But whatever we did
it leaked away,
like water seeping through
a crack in a dam.
It was gone before we knew it,
over and out, like a friend
who couldn't stay.
It slipped off home
and there was no way
we could keep it,
or persuade it to remain.
Then another whole year
before it reappeared.

And oh how we wanted it back,
and oh how we needed it back.
That one day in the dullest year
when anything seemed possible.

Instead

Instead of an X-box
please show me a pathway that stretches to the stars.

Instead of a mobile phone
please teach me the language I need to help me speak with
angels.

Instead of a computer
please reveal to me the mathematics of meteors and motion.

Instead of the latest computer game
please come with me on a search for dragons in the wood
behind our house.

Instead of an e-reader
please read to me from a book of ancient knowledge.

Instead of a digital camera
please help me remember faces and places, mystery and
moonbeams.

Instead of a 3D TV
please take me to an empty world that I can people with my
imagination.

Instead of electronic wizardry
please show me how to navigate the wisdom inside of me.

The Skeleton in the Cupboard

I heard my mother say
that the lady across the road
had a skeleton in her cupboard.

Immediately, of course,
I wanted to see it,
to rattle its bones,
to run my fingers
over its ribcage.

I wanted to snap its jaw,
to touch its teeth,
to make its feet
hit the floor
in a clitter-clatter
of bone on board.

But when I asked
the lady across the road
if I could see the skeleton
in her cupboard,
she wasn't pleased at all,
she shooed me away.

And when I told my mum
that I'd asked
the lady across the road
if I could see
the skeleton in her cupboard,
she wasn't pleased either.

I'm not allowed out now, mum says.
So instead, I'm searching our cupboards
trying to find some whitened bones
of our own.

*(To have 'a skeleton in your cupboard' means to have a secret in your
past that you probably wouldn't want people to know about.)*

Can't

My mum used to say,
take the 't' out of 'can't' and you 'can'.
Or sometimes' she'd say,
'There's no such word as can't.'
But I've found things I can't do.....

I can't lick my nose with my tongue,
I can't bite my toenails,
I can't give the kiss of life to a dead beetle,
I can't scratch my ear with my foot
like my dog can,
I can't keep money in my piggy bank
without spending it,
I can't do the splits like my sister can,
I can't predict with any accuracy
what Tottenham will do at the weekend.
(They sometimes surprise me, mostly dismay me!)

Take the 't' out of 'can't' and you 'can'
my mum said.
But I've got news for her,
however hard I try,
however hard I want to
believe her,
there are still some things
I just can't do.

Winning the Lottery

Our Mum says she's going to win
the lottery.
We keep telling her she's got more chance
of becoming Queen of England
but she never listens.
"Don't want to be greedy," she says,
"A million will do."
"Buy a house, have a holiday or two.
I'm tired of Spain," she says,
"I want a cruise, and a car
that's new and not used."
She says she wants a new wardrobe too
but we can't see anything wrong
with the one dad brought back
from the Pine Shop.
"I'd give money away," she says,
"Give some to charity."

So every time she fills her car with petrol
she's at it, scratching the scratch cards,
buying the tickets. "It's my dream,"
she says, "Everyone needs a dream."

We asked our Dad
why he doesn't play the lottery too,
double our chances.
Dad says he doesn't need new clothes
and a cruise doesn't bother him.
"Besides, I won the lottery once,
the day I married your Mum."

Potpourri
(pronounced 'po pourri')

Bowls of potpourri
keep appearing
all over our house.
Mum says it makes the house smell nice
but Dad says it makes it smell like
an explosion in a perfume factory.
I have to agree.

My brother says it's not potpourri
but potpooey!
He holds his nose as he hurries by.

In the living room it's clove and nutmeg,
in the bathroom it's apple cider and snowdrops
and in the downstairs loo
it's frosted vanilla and fig.

Our dog tries to eat the stuff,
Heaven knows what he finds attractive about it.

I wouldn't mind if you could buy
potpourri that smelt of fish and chips
or egg and bacon or chocolate.
But as you can't
I have to admit that for once
my little brother is right -
Potpouri is definitely potpooey!

The Only Explanation

The fairies must have taken my brother,
swapped him soon after he was born,
left us some wriggly nasty thing
that screams from sundown till dawn.

He laughs when things go wrong
and yells when everything's fine.
He grabs all the food from the table
and steals what's left of mine.

He's an impish creature, with a face
that twists to a horrid shape.
His voice is a devilish babble
and it's something we can't escape.

But my parents don't seem concerned
when I say what the fairies have done.
They beam at him and smile
and never notice what he's become.

When he isn't screaming and bawling
you can hear him whimper and whine.
Yes, the fairies have taken my brother
and what's left is no brother of mine.

Sumo

I know what I want to do
when I grow up and leave school,
I want to be a Sumo.

Not for me a life at sea
or training to fly a jumbo jet.
A Sumo wrestler is what I'll be.

And yesterday,
I went into training.

I ate three bags of chips,
five chocolate bars
and several super size
sandwiches
with bread thick as doorsteps.

I've also taken up meditation
since I heard one Sumo say
that it clears the nasty thoughts
from your head.

And I'm building a ring in the yard.
There'll be no girls allowed inside
once it's finished.

But when my baby brother
waddles around with his nappy on,
with his podgy arms and his chubby legs,
he looks far more Sumo than I do.
It's just not fair!

Why?

"Why did we take off the bathroom door,
to release my little sister?
Why didn't we leave her
stuck in the loo?
We could have kept her there
for a year or two,
we could have used
the other bathroom downstairs.
We could have forgotten
all about my sister.
Life would have been so wonderful,
if we could have lived without her!"

The Babysitter

"We won't be home late," Mum said,
"You'll be all right with the babysitter."

We'd never seen her before,
she looked nervous.

"Would you like to see Boris, my pet rat?"
I asked.

She shuddered,
whispered, "No."

I told her about the programme I saw on TV
where they cut through someone's brain.
"Bit like the Egyptians," I added,
"Pulling out your bits before
they embalmed you."

"We learnt that at school," I said.
She didn't seem impressed.

"Last term we did the Plague,"
I told her.

"If you caught it you'd have boils
all over your body with yellow pus
leaking out."

"Actually, that was what happened
in the horror film we watched
last time Mum and Dad went out
and left us alone with
the babysitter."

"And the best bit was when they took
an eye out of a jar
and cut it up......"

****

'Were you OK with the babysitter?"
Mum asked when they returned.

"She was just like the last one,
disappeared into the bathroom
soon after you left.
We haven't seen her since."

Nothing to do

(Young lad on a bench in Broad Oak, looking bored)

There's nothing to do
but to sit on a seat and think
of what there is to do
when there's nothing to do.

If I had James Bond's yacht
I could sail the Indian Ocean
with a tanned and fit girl at my side.

If I had a rock star's limousine
I'd be with a model or a beauty queen
who'd think that I was just the most
fantastic guy she'd ever seen,
instead of sitting here on a bench
thinking of what there is to do
when there's nothing to do.

If I had a footballer's money
I'd fly my own private jet,
with a footballer's wife calling me 'pet'
and a millionaire's mansion
with a wild jacuzzi and a swimming pool
and some millionairess thinking I'm cool.

But the only girl who comes past
reckons I'm a geek, some sort of freak
sitting on a bench thinking
of what to do when there's nothing to do.

A Different Language

I wish I could lose the silence in me.

I wish I could be the me who wins,
the me who fights for what I want.

I wish I could be the me who pushes words past my lips,
who speaks in tongues of flame
so that the words I say
would burn their way
into your heart.

But I don't understand the language of girls,
it's different to the one I speak.

Geographical Tongue

When I went to the doc
he told me I'd got
a geographical tongue.
'It looks like a map
with mountains and valleys,
it's how I tell there's something wrong.'

'Well I've got historical eyes,' said Mum,
'We've seen a lot, these eyes and me,
they've recorded events
in my history,
my life story, precious to me.'

'And I've got scientific knees,' said Gran.
'They've carried out all kinds
of tests on me,
made grand discoveries about my knees,
the doctors say they're pleased with me.'

'And I had mathematical spots,' said Dad,
'That time when I had chicken pox,
but each day that passed
took some away.'

And I wondered what else
I might have in my life...

artistic ankles,
        musical muscles,
biological bones,
        technological toenails...

After all, anything's possible
with a geographical tongue.

Shaggy Dog!*

When I was a boy,
a bigger boy once convinced me
that there was a crocodile
down my toilet.
This worried me for weeks,
I dared not linger
for fear that some armour plated snout
and a mouth full of wicked teeth
was about to snap
at my bottom.

My parents told me,
"get wise to him,"
there are no crocodiles
in the plumbing
of housing estates.
My mates laughed,
said I was crazy,
I'd have to be
to believe
a story like that.

But whenever I sat
on our toilet seat
I still got worried
and rightly so it seemed
when years later I read
about a snake that escaped
in a skyscraper block
in New York,
and how someone heard knocking
in their toilet bowl,
then lifted the lid
to reveal.....

absolutely nothing!

Well you'd have to be
as gullible as I was
to believe that.
Wouldn't you?

*A shaggy dog story is one that gets you really interested and
then disappoints you at the end.*

Medusa's Bad Hair Days

Although she's tried
every kind of shampoo
nothing works
on Medusa's hairdo.

Her snakes are always
in a tangle,
coiling and spitting
at every angle.

They won't keep quiet,
they won't stay still,
these bickering serpents
are making her ill.

She needs a hero
to hack at her hair,
someone her flickering tongues
won't scare.

A hero willing
to take a chance,
to cut and to kill
without meeting her glance.

A blindfolded hero
acting alone,
someone whose bones
won't turn to stone.

And she's vowed that she'll change
her reptilian ways
if someone can rid her
of bad hair days.

She'll change from the woman
you love to hate,
if someone would ask her
out on a date.

(Are you brave enough
to fall in love
with Medusa?)

Diogenes

(Diogenes was a Greek philosopher who begged for a living and slept in a large pottery jar in the market place in Athens.)

Bit of a squeeze for Diogenes
inside his pottery jar.

Wedged in tight, snail-like,
he couldn't move very far.

Couldn't walk from room to room
or plan any DIY.

Couldn't pop down to the shops
and seek out furniture to buy.

Couldn't invite a friend to stay
and say there's plenty of space.

Couldn't say, just step inside
while I take care of your case.

And didn't you freeze, Diogenes,
in the winter without any heat?

And didn't people think you were crazy
when they passed you on the street?

And what did you do in the middle of the night
when you needed to use the loo?

Sounds crazy to me, Diogenes,
I'm glad I'm me and not you.

Battlefield

(There are different opinions these days as to where the Battle of Hastings actually took place. One opinion is that it was fought where a road and a roundabout now stand.)

This place could be
the battlefield.

This could be the place
where Harold's army,
tired and footsore,
stood their ground
as William's army
bore down on them.

And it isn't hard to imagine
the ranting and roaring,
the flutter of pennants,
the pounding of hooves,
the clashing of swords,
and the frightened steeds
trampling warriors.

And then when it seemed
the battle might be won,
William's army feigned retreat.
History records how a shower
of arrows fired in the air
left Harold dying, his troops
leaderless.

It was all so long ago,
so many memories in the mist,
so many summers, frozen winters.

Who really cares if it was fought
elsewhere?

Yet I hear it still,
down the ages, drawn like the wind
in the wires.

But who will hear it
in years to come,
buried beneath layers of earth,
silenced by the thunder of wheels?

Those 1066, Battle of Hastings Re-enactment Blues

I drew the short straw
for the role I would play,
which meant that I spent
the best part of my day
lying flat on my back
stretched out in the mud,
too close to a cowpat
and streaked with fake blood.

And I've got a feeling we're going to lose.
It's those 1066, Battle of Hastings re-enactment blues.

It's like supporting Tottenham
and knowing you always lose
to Man.U. at Old Trafford
and then suddenly there's news
that totally unexpectedly
the score's 3-2 to you,
and you think if that can happen
maybe this can happen too.

But I've got a feeling we're going to lose,
it's those 1066, Battle of Hastings re-enactment blues.

And I'm hoping that maybe today
us Brits could even win,
that the arrow could miss Harold's eye
and the French army swiftly give in.
If only for a day we could
reverse the course of history,
send the French off home
and celebrate a British victory.

But I've got a feeling we're going to lose,
it's those 1066, Battle of Hastings re-enactment blues.

And really I know it won't happen,
the fatal arrow will still fly by
with Harold's name written on it,
heading straight for his eye.
And that will be the signal
for British soldiers to retreat,
a hoof print on my thigh
as I contemplate defeat.

And I know for sure that we're going to lose,
(and I wish I'd worn more sensible shoes)
it's those 1066, Battle of Hastings re-enactment blues.

According to Traffic Reports...

According to traffic reports
it's STICKY at junction 5
on the M25....

I imagine a long spill of treacle,
cars like flies on
sticky flypaper,
tyre trails criss-crossing
the sticky stuff,
drivers huff-puffing at yet
another delay.

I often hear that
it's TRICKY at junction 3
on the M23.

I imagine magicians hoodwinking drivers,
conjuring illusions,
making roads go
where roads normally don't
then vanishing again
leaving motorists stuck
in fields.

I often hear that
it's LIVELY
at junction 6
on the M26.

I imagine a party
with everyone dancing away
the delay,
lots of hugs and high fives,
car horns hooting,
tooting tunes.

I often hear that
it's sluggish
on the M1.

Now that really does

s   t   r   e   t   c   h

the imagination.

Multi-Storey Car Parking

Can't find a space on the first floor,
can't find a space on the second floor.
The space on the third floor's too small,
between a Vauxhall Vectra and the car park wall.
Can't find a space on the fourth floor,
can't find a space on the fifth floor.
The space on the sixth floor's too narrow,
My car's fat like a garden marrow.
Can't find a space on the seventh floor,
can't find a space on the eighth floor.
The space on the ninth floor's just right,
not too tiny and not too tight.
And I zoom across to the pay and display
where I find I haven't got any money to pay.
So I drive back down to the eighth floor,
and I twist and I turn down seven more
then out in the open and onto the street,
I can't face it anymore I feel deadbeat
till suddenly I see a space that's free
and I turn in quickly but fail to see
twenty minutes parking time only!

Abandoned Car

How good it was to find
an abandoned car in the woods.

It was every boy's dream
and every parents' nightmare,
somewhere dangerous to discover
how easily we could get hurt.

Fingers jammed in a door
that slammed shut,
rusted metal that easily cut
young skin.

But the steering wheel
could still be moved
and the wheels still swiveled
as if they were turning,

turning into the sort of chase
where you were out there,
keeping pace with winners
in a world-class race,

then sneaking past
on the final bend
to claim your champion's kiss
from an anxious girlfriend.

But sadly, soon, reality hit,
this was not the Brazilian
Grand Prix,

just a wreck, jammed tight
between trees,
gone nowhere
for years.

Screaming in Underground Car Parks

In the twilight time
before it's properly dark,
with the odd car still parked
waiting collection,
we're down there
bringing the night to life,
screaming in underground car parks.

Like a pack of werewolves
suddenly loose
our screams bounce about
from the roof to the floor
and anyone calling to claim their car
will shiver when they hear
how noisy we are,
screaming in underground car parks.

And Ricky who lets rip
a dream of a scream
so frightens some car fetching
husband and wife
that they change their minds
and flee.

While hordes of us down there
do crazy tricks
on scooters and skateboards
getting our kicks,
a gang of orang-utans
looting and shrieking,
screaming in underground car parks.

Reasons Why Your Train Was Late This Morning

The train on platform one
had a note from its mum.

The train on platform two
went up in a puff of smoke,
someone said *you know who* was on board.
Don't say his name,
it may not be a joke.

The train on platform three
stopped for a cup of tea,
a sandwich, a cake and two bags of crisps,
then went for a dip in the sea.

The train that should have been on platform four
found a secret door to another dimension,
now it's millions of light years away.

The train on platforms five, six and seven,
came in sideways.

You missed the train on platform eight,
it left already, you were late.

Night Train to Transylvania

On the night train to Transylvania
you can
check out groovy graveyards you may have missed
on previous trips.
You can talk to estate agents about buying
your very own mausoleum
where you'll sleep soundly by day
and then easily escape from at night.
Discuss with other like minded creatures
the best ways to frighten victims,
how to trick them to bare their necks.
Learn different types of bites
and which will give you the deepest drink.
Discover the comfiest coffins
in which to lie for all eternity.
Be warned in advance of the tricks and paraphernalia
of the vampire hunter, of the ways to combat garlic
and avoid a sharpened stake.
You'll meet and mingle with many denizens
of the darkest night, with ghouls and gremlins,
werewolves and warlocks,
so be warned,
that little old lady might be Grand High Witch,
that buffet car attendant could easily
be Count Dracula's descendent
and even that hairy porter could be Voldermort,
(just don't speak his name)
on the night train to Transylvania.

In the Hollywood Lost Property Box

In the Hollywood Lost Property Box
are.....

Superman's tights,
Dorothy's red shoes,
Mary Poppin's umbrella
and one of Jaws lost teeth.

E.T's borrowed bicycle,
Luke Skywalker's light sabre,
Cruella de Vil's wig
and a ticking clock
(inside a crocodile)

Lassie's collar,
Zorro's mask,
Indiana Jones' hat
and one of Robin Hood's arrows.

Frankenstein's bolt,
Peter Parker's spectacles,
Lone Ranger's saddle
and the key to Batman's batmobile.

Tarzan's loincloth,
Cinderella's glass slipper,
Dracula's fangs
and a Caribbean pirate's cutlass.

Please call and collect
or any Items remaining
at the end of the day
will be given away
to charity shops
in L.A.

Cable Cars (San Francisco)

Like all great journeys, you ride
at a risk
on the line down from Powell to Hyde.
No smooth glide
just jerky jumps and then
sliding to a stop for the lights.
The brakeman works his own kind of magic
with the levers
as the streets turn upwards then down.
It's a roller coaster ride
of a town
when you're hanging on
and hanging on some more.

San Franciscans, of course,
know the score,
do it daily.
But for those of us new to this city
it's just the wildest, most exhilarating ride,
one moment looking down
at the rails
and next
gazing up at the stars.

*(Most times when I travel I'm hoping for a seat but
on San Francisco's cable cars, all I wanted to do was to
hang on at the edge!)*

Condor

(Grand Canyon, Arizona.)

You just can't whistle up a condor
from the Canyon,
they don't appear on demand.
That sort of magic
sneaks up on you,
surprises you
when your eyes are held
by Canyon colours,
the greens and the rust,
the bluest of skies.
When you're drawn to the drops
and the hide 'n' seek river,
It's then that something
will catch your eye,
the magic in black and white.
The flight of a bird
like some ancient Navaho apparition,
a feathered god, god of the sky,
now suddenly
brought back to life.

And then much later
when the holiday's done,
and the grey November days
signal summer has gone.
It's then that you'll stop
and remember
the touch of the Arizona sun.
and like a magician
you'll conjure up
the Canyon and the condor.

Vertigo

I'm a seagull that suffers from vertigo.
All the other sea birds think I'm sad
just skimming the waves down below,
it's something that makes me mad.

All the other sea birds think I'm sad
as they see me fly at low levels.
It's something that makes me mad,
to me they're such daredevils.

As they see me fly at low levels
I'm the subject of their scorn.
To me they're such daredevils
while I'm barely even airborne.

I'm the subject of their scorn
as I see them rising with ease
while I'm barely even airborne
hardly disturbing the breeze.

As I see them rising with ease
I'm a seagull that suffers from vertigo,
hardly disturbing the breeze,
just skimming the waves down below.

Bat

A bat had the audacity
to slip in through
the restaurant window,
swooping low over bowls
of soup, then looping the loop
round chandeliers, tiny
bat ears echo-locating,
all the waiters hating
the confusion it creates.
Diners with toupes hold
hands to their hair,
scared faces thinking
they might have to leave
their places and run.
Great fun for the children,
bored by the wait between
courses, or caught with
a fork between plate
and mouth, gazing
amazed, till this
flip-flap of velvet,
this scrap of black
is drawn back out,
to the ebb
and flow
of sky.

The Alien Barbecues

A heavenly pong that we just couldn't trace
had been drifting around up here in space,
till our saucers returned with wonderful news -
it's the smoke from your back garden barbecues.

They smell saucy, spicy and appetising,
scrumptious and luscious, quite tantalising,
delightful, delectable, delicious it's true,
succulent, savoury, nutritious too.

So we've been sent to discover more
of this fast food formula that we can't ignore,
for we've cooked it ourselves and we can't get it right
and that's why we keep calling round every night.

It looks munchable, crunchable, truly scrummy,
gorgeous, mouth watering, chewy and yummy.
It tickles out tastebuds, our tongues become tangled
but we can't get it right and our nerves are now jangled.

For all we have fed on for many light years
are red planet slugs kebabbed on small spears
like the party sausage you eat from a stick
but we're telling you now, they're making us sick.

They're slimy, they're yucky, disgustingly green,
the vilest of creatures you'll ever have seen.
They're stinky and laced with a vinegary taste,
gungey and gooey like smelly fish paste.

So please help us out, we're really uptight,
tell us the secret, we'll get out of your sight.
We won't invade, we'll turn around and go
once you've revealed what we need to know.

And when we're quite sure that we've got it right
we'll invite you to Mars for a fantastic night.
Red planet slugs you just won't refuse
when they're grilled on our alien barbecues.

Musical Fruit

Imagine fruit that sings to you
before you eat it!

Imagine bananas
bringing you a lilting reggae tune
from the Caribbean

or oranges
rocking and rolling around the room.

Imagine a watermelon
shrieking out some heavy metal

or a plum
whistling a Beethoven symphony.

Grapes could form a choir,
a pair of pears could sing harmony.

Tangerines
could do mean Elvis impersonations
while kiwi fruits do karaoke to Kylie.

Imagine opera
brought to you from the fruit bowl,

limes, strawberries, raspberries, cherries
all making merry with Mozart.

How marvellous it would be
hearing such healthy cacophony!

Glitterbread

I'm so bored with pitta bread
I want glitterbread.

Bread that gleams when it catches the light,
bread that glows like the stars at night,

Bread that sparkles then starts to shimmer,
bread that dazzles and never grows dimmer,

Bread that lights my way back home,
bread that shines like a precious stone

I want glitterbread all the time,
something unique, totally mine.

The Celtic Cat

(I don't know if there is any connection between cats and dragons in Celtic mythology, I suspect not. But it would be interesting if there were.)

The Celtic Cat is familiar with dragons,
It knows their secrets, has visited their lairs.
It has admired itself in the mirrored shields
of dragons' treasure troves.
It has singed its tail and whiskers
in the heat of their fire.

The Celtic cat travels to the places
where dragons gather. It would willingly
surrender the lives it has
for an offer of eternity.
And yet, there is already much of the dragon
in the cat itself - a hologram of flame
in its eyes, claws that could rip a hole
in the fabric of our world, through which
myths and memories pour out.

The Celtic cat understands that once,
dragons knew everything -
it desires that knowledge for itself.
A dragon's tongue, dragon's teeth, a dragon's heart,
soon they will belong to the Celtic cat,
and the cherished secret of flight revealed
from the deepest wells of a dragon's soul.
For this is its birthright, it's destiny,
cat and dragon, one and the same,
eyes, wings, dragon flame.....

Talking to the Dog

Home alone, I used to talk to myself,
but now I talk to the dog.
What I say must be really boring because
when I talk to the dog
she falls asleep.
She won't ever struggle to stay awake,
intrigued, perhaps, by what I have to say.

Every day it's the same, of course,
the force of my argument never sways her.

She has her own opinions
of the people who people her patch,
her own ideas about the neighbourhood maps
that she's piecing together,
the fair weather spaces,
the places to go when it rains,
the dogs that bark
when we pass by.

I'd be happy to discuss these too
but I might as well recognise
that I'm a boring sort of guy,
and go back to talking
to myself.

There are just too many barriers between
the dog's agenda and mine.

A Dog shouldn't have to Jog (New York)

A dog shouldn't have to jog
round Central Park on a Sunday.
A dog shouldn't have to run behind
his master's flying feet.
A dog needs time to sniff the air,
a dog needs time to stand and stare,
to meet and greet, to wonder how
other dogs are just allowed
to stroll and take the time they need.
A dog when free and off the lead
should follow his nose and not be tied
by invisible threads to his master's heels,
having no time to give dogs the eye.
With one brief look it's hello and goodbye,
can't stop, I'm off, maybe see you later,
be back round when our circuit's done.
No fun for a dog that has to jog
round Central Park on a Sunday.

Our Dog Chases.....

Our dog chases....

cows	(courageously)
squirrels	(spectacularly)
birds	(creatively)
rabbits	(ravenously)
pheasants	(particularly)
seagulls	(wishfully)
foxes	(fitfully)
bees	(dangerously)
frogs	(occasionally)
chickens	(enthusiastically)
sheep	(rarely)
herons	(unsuccessfully)
and	

CATS of all kinds,
   wherever & whenever
         she can!

No Ordinary Street

I want to live in Polecat Alley,
I want to live in Dead Dog Lane,
don't want to live in an ordinary street
with some ordinary name.

I want to live in Mermaid Rise,
I want to swap my feet for a tail.
I want to hop all the way to Frog Street
and wait each day for my snail mail.

Don't want to live on East or West Street,
don't want to live on North or South.
I want a street that yells out loud,
a street that shoots off it's mouth.

I want to live in Dragon Crescent,
see the night lit up by fire.
I want to live in Phoenix Close
see new life rise from a funeral pyre.

What a pain it would be to live on School Lane,
a complete disaster, no fun at all.
But Dreamland Drive, that would be something,
surf and sunshine wall to wall.

Don't want to live on East or West Street,
don't want to live on North or South.
I want a street that yells out loud,
a street that shoots off it's mouth.

I want to go mad in Crazy Lane,
lose my head in Boleyn Place.
On Harebeating Drive I don't think I could
give overgrown rabbits a punch in the face.

Dumpton Road would leave me depressed,
on Cross Street I'd grumble and grouse.
But Unicorn Avenue, that would be magic,
the perfect place to have my house.

Don't want to live on East or West Street,
don't want to live on North or South.
I want a street that yells out loud,
a street that shoots off it's mouth.

I want to live in Polecat Alley,
I want to live in Dead Dog Lane,
don't want to live in an ordinary street
with some ordinary name.

(All the names of streets mentioned in this poem actually exist
and I actually lived on Harebeating Drive for 7 years!)

World's End*

Anyone living in World's End
must be used to impending doom.

No one makes plans for the future,
no one calls out, "See you next week,"
because no one is certain
that they'll see next week.

No one buys lottery tickets,
no point if the world's ending soon.

I wouldn't want to live in World's End,
wouldn't want to be reminded each day
how fire & flame & tidal wave
could take my life away.

And everyone's wondering what it will be like,
the world when it ends.

Will skies crack open
and a fire burst through?
Will the oceans boil and bubble?
Will the pavements split and buckle?

I just don't want to risk World's End,
I'd rather stay safe where I am.

* *There are villages called 'World's End' in Hampshire,*
Berkshire & Buckinghamshire.

Something Wrong

Opening up the hen house
it's obvious something's wrong.

One chicken's in the nest box,
stiff to the touch.
Our first casualty
in eighteen months
just had to be Dora.

Night time too,
cold January.
Closing them up for the night
I wasn't prepared.

Dora who gobbled sunflower seeds
till she squawked and hooted
like a blocked trumpet.

Dora who grew fat
on a diet of wriggly things,
who caused a riot in the garden
when she raced like a scrum half
with a slow worm.

And I always thought
how good it was to have
a long, long garden,
till I took that walk
back from the black
towards the light.

Holding my secret,
hugging it close.

At that moment,
no one else knowing
that Dora was dead.

Finding A Waterfall

All this time I dog-walked
and didn't know
about the fierce flow of water
in these woods.

All these rainy weeks
must have set it in motion,
this noisy commotion,
this confusion of sounds,
springing from rocks
to surprise us
this Christmas time.

The silvery flow
of this singing stream
now played on by winter sun.

After all those mundane walks
in the rain, there's a waterfall
unlooked for and unexpected.

We stayed there for ages,
the dog and I,
not hurrying at all
to leave.

Zoo of Winds

Wild winds have escaped tonight,
and like animals suddenly loose from a zoo
they are out doing damage.
We hear them snaking
into cracks and crevices
while beasts
with the strength of buffaloes
batter the building.
Shrill birds whistle through the hallway
and a lion's roar seems stuck
in the chimney.
A howling hyena is caught
in the porch
while a horrid hook of a claw
tries to splinter the loft hatch.
All manner of fearsome creatures
lunge down the lane
while our garden is buffeted
by the angry breath of bears.
I hope someone soon
recaptures these beasts,
locks them away,
cages them tightly.
These winds are not welcome visitors,
not tonight, not any time.

The Dinosaur Next Door

I'm in love with the dinosaur next door,
she's a really fabulous creature with an operatic ROAR.
She's the loveliest, most talented dinosaur on our street
and she shimmers like a diamond on a pair of sparkling feet.

Yes, I'm in love with the dinosaur next door
but our love must be a secret, something we must both ignore.
For she's already married to a sharp tooth carnivore
who is handy with his muscles, but she thinks him quite a bore.

He really isn't known for his charm and sensitivity,
in fact his speciality's a certain proclivity
to first rip you to shreds and then ask questions later,
in fact he would be perfect as an armoured gladiator.

So we take romantic walks, my dinosaur and I,
and I hold her claw in mine as we watch the world pass by
while I tell her she should leave him and spend her life with me
but she's frightened that he'd kill me if ever she'd agree.

So I spend my time alone, mostly in misery,
as I think about my dinosaur and what
isn't meant to be.
My future looks cold and bleak since
she's stolen my heart
and like Romeo and Juliet we're
doomed to be apart.

lonelydinosaur.com

lonelydinosaur.com
has just appeared on the world wide web.
And up until now there's never been
a place for those who escaped extinction
to meet and date and possibly mate.
But now there's a dating agency
with all sorts of dinosaurs on its books,
where looks are unimportant
and what really matters is personality,
how much charm one creature
can offer another.

So dinosaurs, wherever you're hiding,
turn on to the new technology,
let them match your details
with dinosaurs on their database.
And before you know it
you'll be out on a date, well on the way
to finding a mate. So take a look
at what's on offer.....

T.Rex would like to meet T.Rex
for friendship or even romance.
Diplodocus needs similar
for social wallowing.
Triceratops needs another
to shop till they drop,
while a lonely velociraptor
would welcome some fun with anyone.
But it isn't considered a good idea
for carnivores to date herbivores
as, 'Nice to meet you' may quickly turn
into 'Very nice to *eat* you'.

But really this is the greatest chance
for dinosaurs to find romance,
for all the lost and lonely ones
who partied too hard
and stayed too long,
who have wandered the world's
most desolate places....
Just get on the net
and find a mate,
call lonelydinosaur.com

Hang-gliding over Active Volcanoes

It was truly amazing the first time I dared
like surfin' in a furnace, but wow, was I scared!
That first time I tried it, I nearly died,
grilled to perfection on the underside.

Yes, I got singed from my eyebrows to my toes
from hang-gliding over active volcanoes.

I saw bubbling lava, fountains of fire,
felt warm blasts lifting me even higher.
I was floating along on waves of steam
while applying layers of suntan cream.

Yes, I got singed from my eyebrows to my toes
from hang-gliding over active volcanoes.

And it didn't take long to get me really hooked
on that great sensation of feeling half-cooked.
What a thrill, I could chill in this situation
if I don't succumb to asphyxiation.

Yes, I got singed from my eyebrows to my toes,
I got scorched from my kneecaps to my nose
from hang-gliding over active volcanoes.

Walking Backwards for Britain

I'm walking backwards for Britain,
Land's End to John O'Groats,
backwards down country lanes
watched only by sheep and goats.

Don't ask me where I'm going,
I concentrate on where I've been,
staring at paths I've followed,
seeing places I've already seen.

Bit of a task walking backwards
making sure that I don't fall down.
Lots of skill required when travelling
backwards from town to town.

It's a challenge, walking backwards,
but it's one at which I excel.
I'm walking backwards for Britain
and I'm doing it rather well.

In the Belly of the Earth

Nobody ever looked inside
the belly of the Earth before.

Nobody ever opened a door
to take a peep within.

For if they had, they would have seen:

A rich and vibrant storeroom
where forgotten flowers
continue to bloom,

where creatures long since disappeared
are living once again,

where dodos and dinosaurs
are seen in great numbers.

They would have seen empty spaces
labelled and reserved.

for tigers and elephants,
for pandas and whales.

And one that really
made us shiver,

'Very Last Human'
soon to be delivered.

For everything that's given
is some day hidden away

Open the door some time,
look for yourself.

Cry for the Moon

"Why do you cry?"
came the question.

"I cry for the Moon," I answered.

"I cry for the Moon's loneliness
as it wanders the sky."

"I cry for the way we abandoned it
to the silence of space."

"I cry for the way it looks,
pock-marked, cratered and dry."

"I cry for the Moon
in that empty sky."

"And if I could, I would try
to write music for the Moon,
to make it merry,
bring a smile to it's face."

"And if I could, I would hang jewels
from the Moon,
make it sparkle,
put fire in it's heart."

"But I can't so instead
I cry for the Moon.

And sometimes
I don't know why

I cry".

Weather Talk

'Biting winds,' the forecaster said,
'There'll be biting winds today.'

But how to biting winds attack,
do they snap at your heels like a yappy dog?
Do they bite your bottom or nip your ears,
do they rip great chunks from your flesh?

Do they scratch your face and leave a mark,
do they act the same way as cold snaps?

And what if you're out in heavy showers,
would they hammer you to the ground?

And what noise does a band of rain make,
surely not a pleasant sound?

And I'd like to know
just what I'd find in pockets of
mist and fog?

Not brilliant sunshine, that's for sure.

An Artist's Touch

We must not be ambitious. We cannot aspire to masterpieces.
We may content ourselves with a joyride in a paintbox -
Winston Churchill (former British Prime Minister)

Let's mix red and green and gold,
let's work with bold colours
and not be shy.
Let's tip up colours till the mix is right,
let's darken the day and lighten the night.

Let's blow bubbles with the blue,
spread fire with the red.
Let's green up grey places
and add yellow to the gloomiest corner.

Let's splash into white
and sky dive purple.
Let's drive on tracks of black.
Let's dance into a sunset glow.

Let's travel on paper to icy wastes,
to desert sands, and vibrant jungles.
Let's create oceans with a wipe of a brush,
a gush of white, a spill of blue.

Let the colours merge, let them flow
into a waterfall of shades
that only we know.

Let's find colours
that no one has found before.

On our joyride in a paintbox,
let's explore......

Pirate DJs

In the 1960s radio stations were set up illegally on ships in the North Sea and 'pirate DJs' broadcast continuous rock music to Britain.

Listen out now for the pirate DJs
as they sail on the airwaves everyday,
hear the rappiest, snappiest music they play
those pirate DJs.

It's the pirate DJs with their stock of treasure,
oldies but goldies to give you pleasure
this isn't work, it's a lifetime of leisure
for pirate DJs.

Just check out the deck and the sounds that they blow
but they won't let you go till you've heard all the show
and they'll talk between tunes till you feel that you know
those pirate DJs.

And they're giving out all kinds of advice
from the evils of weevils to cooking with rice
and the best way to rid your body of lice
those pirate DJs.

Those pirate DJs most days feeling unwell
playing rock as they roll with the North Sea swell
they're magicians who'll have you under their spell
those pirate DJs.

And of course they're much braver than ever we think
they'd keep spinning discs if their ship should sink
till the waters rolled over them, black as ink
those pirate DJs.

Then down on the sea bed you'd still hear them play
rocking the rocks while the sounds ricochet,
from Amsterdam to the Bay of Biscay
those wonderful, wonderful pirate DJs.

Titanic

The stories of heroism live on
through the tales of those who were saved,
but who knows, when faced with such terror,
how anyone would have behaved.

Titanic, they said, was unsinkable,
no way could this ship go down.
It was something that would never happen
to this palace, this floating town.

But four days out of Southampton
when an iceberg gashed the ship,
those left on board knew they'd suffer
the water's icy grip.

So remember those who stepped back
saying, "You first, I'll stay and wait."
"I won't need this," said Mrs. Strauss,
handing a shawl to her maid.

Astor, Strauss, Guggenheim,
all heroes of that ship,
and the band that kept on playing
as the deck began to dip.

And I wonder what I would have done
when faced with such desperation?
Would I have taken that one step back
and abandoned my own salvation?

Or would I have rushed for the lifeboats
escaping that fateful trip,
making sure I was one of the lucky ones
to abandon that stricken ship?

More Things You Can Do or Say to Places in the UK*

You could sing in Tring
or go dancing in Lancing.
Amble round Amble,
go frantic in Frant.
Utter yells in Wells
or be dull in Hull.
But don't mouth off in Louth.

You can jump for joy
with the Old Man of Hoy.
Be cool in Poole (or Goole),
tittle-tattle in Battle.
But it's hell in Pwllheli
when there's nothing
on the telly.

You can 'oller in Ollerton
or wail in Walesby,
say good day to St Mary's Bay
or argue the toss in Kinross.
But you don't want to
lift the lid on Lydd.

(And don't make Dover
fall over,
or poke Hay-on-Wye
in the eye!)

An earlier poem of mine called 'All the Things You Can Say to Places in the UK,' obviously wasn't. There's more.....)

River Don

How fortunate is Don
to have a river named after him.
I wish I had something
named after me.
River Brian doesn't sound quite right,
nor does Brian Street or Brian Road.
(There was a Brian Close once
but he was a cricketer.)
Scotland do interesting things with names.
I'd love to be the Pass of Brian
or the Bridge of Brian - that sounds good.
The name Brian means strength,
tough as cowhide, strong as iron;
maybe I could be the Mountain of Brian.
If I wanted it to reflect the very core of me,
the very heart, if I wanted it to conjure up
the very Brianess of Brian,
I'd find the River Brian flowing in my veins,
Fortress Brian in the heart of me,
Church of Brian in my soul.
And in my eyes, The Great Fire of Brian,
to be glimpsed by everyone
and admired!

A Difficult Poem to Read Unless You've Swallowed a Dictionary

Regalia, Westphalia, saturnalia, paraphernalia.
Potato, tomato, tornado, winnebago.
Technology, tautology, chronology, archaeology.
Vernacular, oracular, spectacular, crepuscular.
Fascinated, anticipated, assassinated, discombobulated.
Now go find words from the dictionary
and string them together just like me.
Let the words tumble, feel them flow,
but is it a poem? Well, who knows?

Temptation

I love standing by the airport carousel
I love that little twitch of fear,
Knowing that with one quick move,
I could change my life,
change somebody else's too.....

Wouldn't it be great
to take someone else's suitcase,
to forget you'd just flown in from Madrid
and lined up for luggage from Rekyjavik instead.
You could take your pick from the carousel,
any one you fancied.
And you wouldn't know if what you'd got
was a better deal, or not,
till you sawed off the lock
and opened the lid.

From all the muddled cases
everyone would take the wrong souvenirs.
Questions would be asked -
why did you buy me
coral from Iceland,
a London taxi from Tenerife,
the Eiffel Tower from Thailand?

But what a chance to shake off a life,
get rid of your past,
a life you'd grown tired of,
throw it away.

Just imagine if everyone took different cases,
wore different clothes, assumed different identities,
how strange it would be......

I was tempted to try, but guess what,
I didn't!

Zzzzzzeds

How much more
could I have done with my life
if I hadn't needed
so many zzzzzeds?
All my shopping done
in all night supermarkets,
all the films
I could have seen,
books I could have read
instead of zzzzzeds,
instead of sleeping away
one-third of my life,
that precious stuff,
short enough as it is.
I could have learned languages,
Serbo-Croat or Japanese,
easy if you don't need sleep.
I could have studied more,
trained hard to be a doctor,
or a fighter pilot.
I could have travelled to places
I never dreamt I'd visit,
if I hadn't needed
so many zzzzzeds.
If I'd filled my head with actions
rather than dreams.
All the schemes, scams,
I could have masterminded,
the quiz programmes I could have
worked at to win.

So tonight I'm going to stay awake,
I'm just not going to sleep,
I'm just not going to sl.......zzzzzzzzzzzzzz.

Space Station 215

This is Space Station 215
letting you know that we're still alive
and kicking, out here at Planet Rock
with DJ Robot, your Cosmic Jock.

We're bringing to you these sounds from space,
sounds that will take you some other place.
We got Androids, Humanoids, Starlighters too,
We got Moondog and Big Star, just for you.

We got a shipload of sounds comin' in today,
flying them fast along the Milky Way,
We got r 'n' b, we got rock 'n' roll,
we got the strangest sounds from a deep black hole.

We got Mercury Rev, we got Moontrekkers too,
We got Sigue Sigue Sputnik comin' to you.
We got all sorts of music to give you a lift,
we're rockin' so hard we'll make your planet shift.

So listen in and listen good
to these sounds we bring to your neighbourhood.
Just turn your radio up to the sky,
we're blasting down from way up high.

This is Space Station 215
letting you know that we're still alive
and kicking, out here at Planet Rock
with DJ Robot, your Cosmic Jock.

In All These Lives...

I've been heroes and heroines,
I've been Queens, I've been Kings.

I've been a foot soldier in the army of Bonaparte.
I've been Romeo having lost his heart to Juliet.
I've been a bare knuckled boxer looking for a fight.
I've been with Harold on the night before Hastings.
I have travelled with Amundsen, with Columbus and Marco
Polo.
I have sailed solo into the eye of a cosmic storm.
I have whispered words into Shakespeare's muddled mind.
I have been a president ordering swift retaliation.
I have ridden as Boudicca's daughter and fought alongside my
mother.
I have witnessed the slaughter of the elephants in the Roman
Colosseum.
I have journeyed as a refugee when my home has been
destroyed.
I have worked on atomic bombs in the desert of Nevada.
I have shaken hands with the ones who imprisoned me.
I've been the general when the peace treaty was signed.
I've been the one who saw and the one who was blind.

Yes, I've been many things and I've been more,
in all these lives that I have lived before.

Your Majesty

(CBBC asked me to write a poem for the Queen's 80th birthday and then perform it live on air. Maybe it's framed and hanging up in one of the Buckingham Palace dog kennels!)

Has anyone thought how the corgis
might celebrate your eightieth year?
If they could write, perhaps with a sonnet
or two, like Will Shakespeare.

Or maybe a twenty-one bark salute
in honour of your eighty years,
or a chorus of musical howls
that are pleasing to royal ears.

But Your Majesty, corgis are limited
in what they can say or do.
So here at CBBC, on behalf of
your dogs - Happy Barkday to you!

The Budgie Likes to Boogie

Brian's poetry never fails to capture the imagination of his many readers. If you are a newcomer to his work or a Brian diehard, this book will have you dancing with glee! These funny and heart warming feather brained rhymes about animals, insects and birds are a real tweet!!

"Brian is one of Britain's favourite children's poets."

(The National Poetry Archive)

The Great Galactic Ghoul

A long time ago in a galaxy far, far away......Brian Moses wrote some poems!! From the first shopping trolley on the Moon to New York City, these universal poems cover most subjects in the universe!!

These out of this world, weird and wacky verses will make you laugh, cry and think....whatever planet you're from!!

Just watch out for the Great Galactic Ghoul........

"A well-loved and acclaimed children's poet."   *(Sunday Post)*

Brian Moses writes poetry and picture books for children and resource books for teachers.

Since 1988, he has toured his poetry and percussion show round schools, libraries and theatres throughout the United Kingdom and abroad.

He has published over 200 books and was once asked by CBBC to write a poem for the Queen's 80th birthday.

You can read interviews with Brian at www. poetryzone.co.uk and at www.authorshotline.com/bmredsea

At www.brianmoses.co.uk you can listen to a selection of poems, watch a film and complete the Brian Moses quiz.

Check out Brian's blog for lots of idea to get you writing your own poems - brian-moses.blogspot.com

Brian can be booked for performances via www.authorsabroad.com

Other books by Brian Moses

The Budgie Likes to Boogie - Brian's poems about animals. (Caboodle Books)

The Great Galactic Ghoul (Caboodle Books)

Python - Brian's first story book. (Caboodle Books)

What Are We Fighting For - New Poems about War - Brian Moses & Roger Stevens (Macmillan)

Behind the Staffroom Door - The Very Best of Brian Moses (Macmillan)

A Cat Called Elvis (Macmillan)

Olympic Poems - Brian Moses & Roger Stevens (Macmillan)

The Monster Sale (Frances Lincoln)

Trouble At the Dinosaur Cafe (Puffin picture book)

The Snake Hotel (Macmillan picture book)

Animal Pants (Macmillan picture book)